Two More Years

A memoir

Two More Years

Tendar Tsering

4

Two More Years

Copyright©2017 Tendar Tsering

All rights reserved, including the right to reproduce this book, or portions thereof in any form.

ISBN-13:978-1545301265
ISBN-10:1545301263

In memory of Kelsang Namtso, 17, who died in an open fire by the Chinese border patrol in 2006, and many others who died in anonymity while crossing the Himalayan border.

1

I was born in 1985 in a small town on the northeastern side of Tibet, where Mao's Great Leap Forward movement was still prevalent. Everything was censored. Everybody was scared of one another. Suspicion ruled. Trust was nonexistent. Almost everyone was living in fear.

My grandparents were victims of the Chinese officials, and so were my parents. We were the black sheep of the nation, because we were born as Tibetans. We were still living in Tibet, but we were indirectly forbidden to recognize ourselves as Tibetans. We were supposed to recognize ourselves as Chinese. And there was a cultural genocide against all the Tibetans. So being born in Tibet in such an era was a tragedy, and being born in a town where there were no signs of modern civilization was bad luck. So, it was my double bad luck to be born in a small town where there were no signs of modern civilization, and to be born in an era of tragedy and misfortune where there was a war against my kind of people.

Whenever we went to the city, we would walk for days. I had been out of our town a few times, and every time, I visited the city, I used to envy the Chinese children in the city playing with toys and running around in their school uniforms. I often wished I had been born as a Chinese, so I could be in that fancy school uniform and play with stuffed bears and toy cars, and wear that red scarf around my neck.

Life in our town was so different, so backward that people didn't have watches or clocks. It was our neighbor's rooster that would tell us the time. He would crow three times in the morning; once around four, then around five and then around six o' clock.

During the day, if we wanted to know the time, we would poke a stick into the ground and the stick's shadow on the ground would tell us the time of the day.

If there was no shadow of the stick, then it was midday. If the shadow fell on the northeastern side, then it was around 1:30 p.m. and if the shadow was on the northwestern side, then it was in between 9 a.m. to noon and so on.

Despite its poor infrastructure and lack of economic development, our town was relatively peaceful, and people were helpful to one another. If a family built their house, almost the entire town would help the family to build the house. They would work for each other for free of cost.

Every night, men and women sat in a semi-circle in front of a hearth. Men would usually recite Buddhist mantras with prayer wheels in their hands, while women would knit.

Almost all of the houses in the town were full of laughter. People loved laughing and telling stories. Most of the stories were about gods and goddesses, but occasionally, they talked about the Tibetan spiritual leader, the Dalai Lama, and the schools that the Tibetan spiritual leader had founded in India for children from Tibet. Stories about the schools seemed too good to be real, but I always wanted to go to India. India was my dreamland. There was no school in our town nor in the neighboring towns. But my father was well versed in the Tibetan language, Bon religion, astrology and mathematics. People said he studied by himself while herding our animals back in his childhood days. He was revered as a Lama even before he became a monk. He became a monk when I was nine. It was a shock to me.

"Your father has become a monk, and he has vowed not to eat meat," said my grandpa when I came home from a hide-and-seek game that I used to play with other children in the town.

My father even had vowed to limit his meals. He ate only twice a day. But he drank milk and ate fruits. The whole town was proud of my father, and they would bring all sorts of fruits to him. The town would treat me as a prince as well.

Until I went to the city closest to our town, I thought my family was the richest family in the world. I used to boast and be arrogant. But as soon as I went to the city, I realized, I was a frog in the well. No one in the city treated me as a prince; rather, they treated me as a beggar. It was all an eye-opening experience, and my desire to study became stronger. But I loved playing with clay, making clay toys of cars and airplanes. I loved toy cars and toy airplanes. I had never seen an airplane other than in the movies. Once a year, a man from the city would come to our town to show movies. In the movies, Chinese actors were always our favorites and Westerners in the movies were always the bad people. When a Chinese person would kill or kick the Westerner, we all would clap and shout, "*Yagthe, yagthe*," meaning "Good, good."

My grandfather was in his 60s and he had different views. His views were unknown to the town. He kept everything to himself, but occasionally, he would tell me, "The Chinese are the bad people. Not the Westerners."

He told me that when he was a child, life was better and much more peaceful. Twisting his head around to make sure no one was listening, he muttered, "Tibet was once an independent nation."

Walking through the town's sea of fields, my grandpa would often show me the fields that once belonged to our family and say, "When Tibet gets freedom, these fields will be ours."

My grandpa and I were mostly out on the mountains, looking after our sheep and goats. He was deeply religious. He loved lecturing me not to shout when we were at the peak of a mountain or near a lake.

"Don't shout. If we shout, mountain gods will become angry," said my grandpa.
He was right. Whenever we shouted, it started raining, or hailing and thundering. And then my grandpa would say we had angered the mountain gods.

I loved being on the mountains, or near the lakes. The scenery was so beautiful, so soothing and so quiet. But, I was a little scared to be near the lakes because when we walked near the lakes, the color of the water changed—from turquoise to a charcoal color.

There were a few places in my hometown that people believed were homes to the spirits who were believed to be the owners of the land. No one dared to cut a tree or branch, or pee in these areas.

While lecturing me not to shout, or pee on these particular mountains, or near a lake, my grandpa often talked to himself. He whispered to the wind and kept telling me that the Dalai Lama in India could hear his messages through the wind. With an incense burning ceremony, he would pray to the mountain gods, and shout, "Free Tibet and long live the Dalai Lama."

I hardly prayed during the ceremonies, but I kept looking up in the sky and shouted when I saw planes flying in the sky, even though I could see only their vapor trails.

2

In our town, women were second-class citizens. Women were traditionally taught to be humble, docile and obedient. They were always obedient to their parents and to their husbands.

Parents in our town would decide the marriages of their children. My parents were keen to get a woman for me. My mom would often tease me. If I was good and worked hard, she would choose a beautiful wife for me when I turned 15. I was shy, and would cry, "I don't want to get married."

Our family had lots of farms, and there was a shortage of workers as two of my uncles decided to have their own families instead of staying in our joint family. My parents wanted me to get married to a woman who would be at least three to five years older than me.

My cousin was the most beautiful girl in our town. She was nineteen. She had long black hair with almond-shaped eyes. She was always smiley and joyful. The dimple on her cheek made every man fall in love with her, and every woman jealous of her beauty.

She was in love with a slim, muscular man, who she said had the heart of a lion and the soul of an angel, but she was forced to marry a nomad guy, who had rosy cheeks, and dark skin with a sea of blackheads on his face. People said her father and the nomad guy's father had decided to let their children marry each other even before they were born.

My cousin was reluctant and resistant even on her wedding day. She banged the doors, punched on the walls. She begged with tears, but her family dragged her down from their house, put her on a horse and started the marriage celebration. The whole town was celebrating as the two richest families in the town were strengthening their bond. I sat in a corner with tears rolling down on my cheeks. My mom gave me a chocolate biscuit, making me smile and join the celebration.

Even after marriage, for months, people said my cousin didn't allow her husband even to lay a finger on her. At last, her husband and husband's father teamed together to let the husband make love to his reluctant wife. My poor cousin was in other words raped. Raped and stuck with her rapist for her entire life. Within a few years, the rapist as I would call him, was the father of her two sons.

That was how my cousin became a lovely wife in that so-called lovely family, one of the most respected and loved families in the town.

Forced marriage was a vicious cycle for many eras, but with the rolling of time, it was on the edge of ending, yet many people in our town were still practicing that tradition of arranged marriage.

3

Every summer, we held yak, bull and sheep fighting festivals. Our family had around sixty sheep, and we had a giant male sheep named *Druk-kar* meaning white dragon.

Our *Druk-kar* was strong, ferocious and elegant. His horns were thick and curved with several folds, and they were as big as Yak horns. *Druk-kar* was my favorite sheep. I would feed him leaves, wheat and barley. My father had made a small special, colorful bag for feeding our *Druk-kar*. I would feed him every day. Sometimes, he would gratefully eat whatever was there in the bag, and at the end, he would step back and then run forward with all his strength and hit me with his curved horns. I would lie flat on the ground crying. He would then simply walk away from me. Possibly that was his way of telling us that he was ready to participate in any sheep fighting festival. After all, he was trained to be wild and violent.

We didn't have any yaks. We had a few horses, bulls, oxen and cows. Each of them had a bell around their neck, and when they were in the jungle, we could recognize them by the sound of their bells.

Usually, they were obedient and didn't need anyone to look after them. We would just open the door of our farmhouse in the morning, and they would go out to eat grass on the meadow or in the jungle nearby and come back in the afternoon.

Our horses were for transport, cows for milk, and we would make butter and cheese out of milk as well. Our oxen were for plowing during cultivation, and the sheep provided wool. We would make pants, coats and blankets out of wool. Everything was homemade. Wool pants were warm and smooth, but I hated anything that was made out of wool. I would purposefully tear my wool clothes whenever my father visited the nearby city, hoping he would buy me a Chinese police uniform. I knew police officers were the most powerful people in the region. They would come to our town occasionally for meetings and sometimes when there were family disputes, or if someone knifed someone else. Everyone feared the officers, and our town would treat the officers with utmost respect with extravaganza shows and meals.

I always wanted to become an officer. But that dream of mine faded away as I realized the town's respect for the officers was fake and out of fear.

One day, around midnight, ten police officers came to our house, yelling and thrashing, kicking around, and shouting at our grandfather. We knew the officers were in the town for an annual meeting, but we never expected a raid on our house.

To our surprise, the officers were drunk and later we learned that they had come directly from a family feast in the town.

One officer handcuffed my grandpa from

behind, forcing him to kneel down, and another officer kicked my grandpa's face from the front. My grandpa was bleeding, and our floor was painted with blood as they kicked, punched and dragged him down to the dining hall. My parents and I begged for forgiveness even before we knew our grandpa's crime. But the officers threatened us with guns in their hands. So, we all stood behind, looking helplessly. The officers asked if we had *chang*, homemade Tibetan beer, and my mother served them the beer. They kept drinking *Chang* and interrogating my grandpa for hours. With tears racing down my cheeks, I told myself, "I don't want to be like them. They are evil. I don't want to be an officer."

My father signaled for me to go inside my room, and I went inside my room, but I could still hear the yelling, slapping, and my grandpa constantly begging for pardon.

My teeth grinding, I kept hugging and wetting my pillow with my tears until I fell asleep.

The next morning, when I woke up, my grandpa was still in the dining hall, drinking his tea. I was glad that he was still there, but my tears rolled down on my cheeks as I saw his face was full of bruises. I hugged him, and asked him, "What did you do?"

He said "nothing."

I looked at my father wondering if he had an answer. He was in deep thoughts and didn't even notice my glance. I looked at my mom. She looked terrified. With her swollen eyes locking onto mine, she patted me on my head and took me away from my grandpa.

"Come here, grandpa has to go," whispered my mother.

Later, I learned that someone in the town had told the officers that my grandpa was a follower of the Dalai Lama and had ideologies that could harm the harmony and unity of the country.

And on the next day that the officers raided our house, my grandpa had to beg for forgiveness in front of all of the people in the town and denounce the Dalai Lama as nothing more than a "monk in wolf's cloth.

4

I always thought my grandpa was the most trustworthy person in the world, but to my surprise, he had never kept my secrets. He had told my secrets to my father. My father knew my desire to go to India to be a student.

One day, not long after I turned into twelve, my father suddenly asked me if I wanted to go to India, and I replied to him, "Yes."
"Do you really want to go to India?" asked my father.

"Yes," I replied.

"Then, you are leaving today," said my father.

For years, I had been hearing about the Tibetan schools in India founded by the Dalai Lama, and I had always wanted to go to India. India was my dreamland. But then, my father's decision was so sudden. Everything was so sudden. My father was all set. Everything was ready. After two hours, my father and I bid goodbye to our family members and relatives.

All of my family members were sniveling except my younger brother who was then three years old. My mother ran after me for fifteen minutes. She was shaking, crying harder than she could control. I was in shock. I had become numb. I told my mother to wipe away her tears and go back. She was holding my hands, constantly kissing them and putting them on her forehead as if I had suddenly become a holy lama.

"It is a suicide decision. You don't have to go if you don't feel like going." My mother was holding my hands, asking me to think twice.

"Mom, I want to go," I took my hands away with my feet stamping on the ground. My mom pulled me back towards her, hugged and kissed me on my forehead. I forcefully took away my hands, and walked ahead with my father.

I looked back, and my mother was still standing on the road, looking towards me.

I waved my hands in the air signaling her to go back home. She turned back and walked towards home. I turned around, and walked ahead with my father. My father was a strong man. He was not crying. I also didn't cry. Like father, like son.

After four days of walking and travelling by a bus, we reached Lhasa, the capital city of Tibet. By then, I noticed my father had become a different person. Every topic that we talked about seemed emotional and his eyes were often welled with tears.

My father even told me why everything was decided in a hurry. He said if he had told me his decision to send me to India earlier, I would have told the news to my friends and that could land us in trouble with the Chinese police.

He was right. If he told me about the decision in advance, I wouldn't have been able to control my excitement and would have told my friends which could land me in jail instead of

India.

Even in Lhasa, everything was fast-forwarded. On midnight of the day after we arrived in Lhasa, we met several other Tibetans, including a few children at a hotel outside the city.

"All of them are going to India, and you will be going with them," said my father.

"Ok," I replied.

My father was restless. He was worried, and he asked me several times if I really wanted to go to India. I was adamant. "Yes." I told him. My father even asked me if I wanted him to accompany me to India. I said, "No".

My father emptied his purse and paid the guide, a man in his early forties. The man didn't sign an agreement but promised to take care of me. Not long after the payment, a wagon came in the driveway of our hotel, and we all jumped in one by one.

My father was standing outside the wagon. So were other relatives or parents of the children and other elders who were leaving Tibet for India.

My father was in tears. He ran towards me and asked me not to go. I replied, "I am going." He was deeply emotional. He uttered some prayers under his breath, and held up my hands on his forehead.

"Get going, get going," shouted the guide. The wagon started moving, my father released my hands, and wiped his tears.

As the wagon zigzagged the streets of Lhasa, I could no longer see my father. Everybody in the wagon was crying. Even the street dogs in the city were mourning and crying. It was a sad, quiet night.

On the second day after we left Lhasa, we reached Shigatse, the second biggest city in Tibet. It was around mid November and winter was already in the air.

We left the wagon behind along with the driver, and started walking ahead. The sky was low and dark. The ground was grey, and the two looked like kissing each other. We could feel the frozen soil beneath our feet, and the cold air on our faces. The air was mild at first but slowly cold enough to numb our faces and extremities.

There were around forty of us, and everybody seemed as if we were in a race. I was carrying a bag, bigger than myself. It was loaded with all kinds of stuff enough to last for a month or so. I felt the straps of the bag, digging deeply into my shoulders, and from time to time, I found myself lagging behind. I knew it was the bag on my back that was making me unable to catch up with the rest of the group. I opened the bag and threw away all the heavy stuff such as woolen blanket, *Tsampa* barley mixed with butter, and yak meat. I kept only the light ones: a cotton blanket, cookies and a couple of ramen noodles. Initially, the elders in my group made fun of me for lightening my bag, but after crossing a few mountains and rivers, everyone seemed to follow my suit. I felt my feet light. I was able to walk in same pace as others, but we had to cross the river, Brahmaputra. It is one of the biggest rivers in Asia. The color of the river was beautiful. It is my favorite— sky blue color. It was a huge river. Fortunately, the place we had to cross the river was split into three slow-flowing channels that made it easy for us to cross the river. But still, it was deep and terrifying. I thought I would die in the river. I looked into the sky. I could not see any planes. It was a wide, clear, empty sky except a few clouds constantly moving in any direction. Sky was always sky. It was the only familiar thing to me.

My thoughts were full of crazy, stupid ideas. I wished I could borrow the moving-clouds from sky to cross the river. But then, within seconds, I was already in the river along with the rest of my group.

 "Hold hands tight," shouted the guide as we walked through to cross the river. I could hardly keep my chin up over the water. I was walking beside a young man in his thirties. He was huge, tall and strong. So I didn't feel the pressure of the gushing river.

A grandmother and a child in the group were floating in the river, but luckily their hands were locked with other elders who were kind enough to risk their lives to save others.

As we came out of the water, we could barely walk. It was too cold. The icy cold water stole heat from every part of our body. We rushed to a nearby cave and hid there for hours.

I took out my blanket from my plastic bag, and wrapped myself up and lay down in the cave. After more than a day, my senses were finally back. Now I knew it was real. The cold was real. The fear was real. Every body around me was a stranger to me. All of them looked so selfish. I was on my own. And I was on a suicide mission. The image of my father crying in the crowd and my mother in tears, standing on the road, started hovering in my mind, making me shed tears. I clenched my fists together, consoling myself, "Be strong, be strong."

As the sun went down along the edge of the river, and dark fell over the area, we resumed our journey, walking towards the border.

5

We walked in the night and slept during the day. This was our strategy to stay away from people. The moment we began our journey, we became people phobia. We hid from everyone. We were scared of anyone who could literally see and speak. We were scared of spies. We were scared of the border patrol.

Walking through the never-ending valley, I came to know why this country is also known as *snow land*. It was hard to find a dry place to sit or sleep on. Crossing the zigzag icy river by the valley, Tashi, our guide shouted, "Don't stop. Keep walking. If you stop, you will be frozen."

It had been three weeks that we had been walking. It was night. I could not see anything further than the person walking ahead of me.

Constantly walking and crawling on the snow, my shoes were frozen. My fingers were numb. I was senselessly walking ahead like a zombie. My mind and my body were a world apart. I could hear the sound of snow ice dangling from the edges of my shoes and pants. And I could even feel my breathing was getting short and shorter, but my mind had been transported back to my hometown— running away from my mom, and refusing to wear the thick, warm wool pants that my mother was trying to put on me.

Then, I heard our guide shouting, "Keep walking, keep walking."

I tried to stop transporting my mind back to my hometown, and tried to be in the present. But my mind was often in the past, enjoying the memories of my time with my family. Here and there, the guide kicked me from behind and pushed me ahead. My feet were also as reluctant as my mind. Tears rolling on my cheeks, I begged our guide to let me go back. He grabbed my shoulder and pushed me away, shouting, "Go."

He kept walking ahead. Everybody was walking ahead. I stood there, lagging behind for a minute, scanning around and looking back and forth. It was dark and scary. I started to run to catch up with the group. No one gave a damn about my decision. By then, everyone knew that I had not much of a choice but to follow the group down the shallow river valley.

For days, we had been following the river down the valley. I never thought that we would have to climb up hills again. Someone once told me that our country was the source of water for most of the Asian countries, including the two giant nations in the region, India and China. So, I was certain that following the river down the valley would lead us to India. But I was wrong.

Following the river was not enough. There were mountains in between which we had to walk up and down. In fact, we climbed several mountains before shadowing the creek down the valley. The mountains that we climbed up and walked down seemed like nothing in comparison to the mountain that was ahead of us. It was huge, tall and fully covered with snow. With the moonlight shining over the peak of the snow mountain, we could see this mountain was not an ordinary mountain. It was standing right next to Mt. Everest, and all the mountains in the region looked like Everest, gigantic and as tall as the sky itself.

"We have to camp here tonight and we will hit the mountain tomorrow morning," said the guide.

"How long does it take to cross the mountain?" asked Tenzin, father of Khando, the child who gave me a chocolate cookie the other day.

"It will take two days," replied the guide.

"Two days?" Tenzin was terrified. Tenzin was in his late thirties. He was strong, brave and short tempered. As usual, he started yelling at the guide.

"How can we climb up this mountain without having anything to eat?" asked Tenzin.

Tenzin and the guide started to yell at

each other. Yelling at each other was a normal routine of our journey. But that night, these two men shouted at each other as if they were going to kill each other.

There were around forty-five of us, and all were strangers to me. I knew none of them. All of them looked selfish. I hated all of them except Khando, who told me that she would be my friend. She was my only friend.

The quarrel between Tenzin and the guide finally led to the decision that we would camp at the base until we got something to eat. The guide said that there was a nomad behind the mountain, and two men from our group volunteered to cross the mountain and bring back some edibles.

We shouldn't have thrown away all the food items if we knew that the journey would take this long. For goddamn sake, can't we just follow the river instead of crawling up the mountain?

My thoughts were full of questions. My mind was full of anger. I started cursing in my mind all of the people that I knew and all of the people that I loved.

I started cursing my father for sending me away from my friends and family. I started cursing my mother for not rejecting my father's decision to send me away. Every night, I asked *"why this?"* and *"why that?"* Regretting my decision to go to India, I wished my parents had forced me not to embark on this risky journey.

I thought I was the best and most obedient child in my family, and I knew it was for my own future, but it was always hard to understand the nature of grown up minds. As long as they could see a good outcome, they could risk anything and everything!

I hated my parents as much as I missed them. Cursing and hating were part of my nighttime routine. After around fifteen minutes of hateful introspection, I wrapped myself up with a cotton blanket that my father had bought for me. I tried to sleep, but it was hard to fall asleep when one was hungry, angry and homesick.

It was always the guide who put my sweet

dreams to an end. It was his style to wake me up by kicking me from behind. In the nighttime, when he would wake me up while I fell asleep while walking, I could see only his teeth; the rest was as dark as the night itself.

On the morning of twenty-sixth day of our journey, our guide did not wake me. I just woke up by myself. The sun was already in the middle of the sky. As usual, it was only the sun that I could recognize with a sense of familiarity. Everything else was strange.

Yawning and stretching my limbs with a twist, I saw the guide and a few others were trying to bury a dead body. I walked closer to the dead body and recognized it was the nun who was in her early 20s. I thought she died as a result of the bitter cold weather, but our guide said she died of hypoxia.

I jumped in and started helping others dig the grave. The ground was frozen. With stones in our hands, we tried to dig up the ground to bury the corpse, but the stones in our hands were not even enough to make a mark on the ground. So, we made a fire out of cow dungs to warm up the ground, and later we were able to bury the body by digging down and covering it up with pebbles and stones. We all started reciting whatever mantras we knew for the dead. We also prayed for ourselves. It was first time for me to see a dead body but I was not scared of the dead body rather I was scared that I also might die like the nun. I prayed, "God, please keep me alive." I could see the fear was palpable on everyone's face. Especially, when we were stranded in a place where there was no wood to make a good fire and no food to fill our stomachs. Khando's father, Tenzin, was an ex-monk, and he started taking refuge in prayers. He kept praying the whole day. I tried to follow his steps but it was hard to focus on reciting mantras. I kept drinking water again and again. My head was spinning. I felt like vomiting, but there was nothing in my stomach to vomit out. Every time that I felt nausea and felt like vomiting, my stomach pained to death. The pain, the hunger and the nausea eventually led to confusion— not knowing if I was still alive or dead or merely having a nightmare. The image of my mom feeding me with her hand also hovered in my mind, making my mouth watery. I missed my mom. I missed my mom's food more. I knew I was alive. I knew I was starving. So, every time, I knew I was alive, I kept drinking water, again and again. I could hear my stomach growling. I leaned forward with my hands on my stomach trying to stop the rumbling noise coming from my stomach. Initially the rumbling brought a few strange stares from my group but later no one bothered to stare at me. Everybody was in the same shoes. Our faces started becoming pale. Our bodies started surrendering to the gravity, making it hard for us to sit straight or lift our limbs up.

Usually, the sun moved so fast from mountain to mountain, but when we were hungry, the sun seemed so still. It was moving like a snail. Now and then, children in the group cried for food, and I could see they were tired and getting weak as much as the elders were getting worried and terrified. All of us were waiting for the two young men who went to the other side of the mountain to get some food for us.

After hours of waiting, the sun finally went down to welcome the night. It was dark, and everyone went to sleep hoping the two men would return the next day.

When we woke up the next day, it was just another fasting day. The whole day, we drank water. The two young men were supposed to return, but they didn't. By then, it was not only me, but almost all of the people in the group were in a panic and regretting taking this unwelcoming, risky journey.

Everybody blamed the guide. Tenzin even threatened to kill the guide if the two volunteers didn't return, and if we were destined to die from hunger.

On the third day, around five in the evening, the two gentlemen returned with a small bag of rice. Everybody shouted in joy. Some even cried and hugged the two men. We cooked the rice and ate around one fourth of it, and saved the rest for the next day.

The Dalai Lama once told a reporter that his favorite food was whatever he ate when he was hungry. He was right. When one was hungry, even rice was more delicious than a meal of a thousand different plates.

Being stranded on the snowy slope was a terrible experience, but the dinner was quite a feast.

The next day, we started our journey around five in the morning. The moment we began our journey, we had to walk up a very steep snowy mountain.

It was still dark and snowing. We could see nothing other than ourselves walking up the hill with our hands chained to each other like a group of ants climbing up a tall stick in the middle of nowhere.

Around seven in the morning, the sun was up and the snow had stopped falling, but everything was clouded. We could hardly see anything. After eight hours of crawling up against the hill, we reached the top of the mountain. It was windy and terrifying, but the wind had overridden the foggy environment. We stood atop of the mountain and raised our hands in the air. We could see everything very clearly, and the scenery at the peak of the mountain with winds making a wave of snowy flakes was worth risking one's life to have such a once in a blue moon experience. The air on the heaven-kissing mountain was chilly and numbing, but the image of the sunshine mixed with mist down the legs of the wide mountain gave us a feeling of ourselves not just being on the top of the world but on the top of heaven.

"*Kyi kyi so so lha gyalo.*" We thanked the mountain god for looking upon us and making our journey safe throughout the long trek. With a semi-smile on his face, the guide shouted, "We are crossing into Nepal now. This will be the last time for many of us to see our own land."

Before sliding and crawling down the hill, we had one last glimpse of *Gya La* Mountain, which is the border of Tibet and Nepal.

In silence, we wept. We even kissed the ground. It was indeed a mixture of feelings, giving one last goodbye kiss to the land of one's birth and entering into an unknown country.

6

After walking for a month, we were finally on the other side of Mt. Everest. We were in Nepal, but people in Samdor village still looked like us. They even ate like us, and dressed like us. They had decorated their houses with Buddhist prayer flags, and almost all of them could speak Tibetan. They were kind and welcoming. I felt as if I were back in my hometown. It was hard to believe that we were in Nepal.

Our guide said the village was a safe place to rest for a day or two. So our group decided to stay there for two days.

Our group was divided into several subgroups, and we were all hosted by the villagers. Along with five others, I stayed in a cattle house. For the whole two days, we kept eating and eating. I ate around ten packages of ready-made noodles. So did the rest of people in our group. During the night, we could hear nothing but our burps, which smelled like rotten eggs.

"Now, I have no regret even if I die tonight," said Tenzin, adding that one shouldn't die of hunger.

Tenzin was funny when everything went as we planned, but his joke that night rather reminded us of the tough days that we went through before reaching Samdor village. However, everybody smiled and laughed as if Tenzin's joke was as funny as it may sound.

There were around fifteen other Tibetans in the village. They had arrived a month earlier than us, but they were still taking refuge in the village. Almost all of them were suffering from frostbite. A boy in the group had lost all of his fingers and his right eye. He was fifteen years old, just three years older than me. The moment their guide said he was alone, my tears somehow rolled down on my cheeks. I felt lucky that I was still alive, still healthy.

A young man in the group had lost his brother while crossing the border. His group said he didn't speak a word thereafter. He was deeply traumatized. When he saw us, he joined our group and told us that his group ditched his brother and him on *Gya La Mountain*. His brother was having headaches, and was unable to walk. He and his brother were left at the peak of the mountain for a week without food.

"We were so hungry that we even ate soil," the young man recalled with tears rolling down on his cheek.

"My brother asked me to eat his flesh and walk ahead, but I stayed with him until he passed away," added the man. He was shaking and trying to calm himself. Through his story, I could see the images of dead bodies that I saw on the way while we were crossing the mountains. All of us could immediately connect to each other. We kept in silence. No one really asked him any questions. The young man also didn't go in detail about what happened to him and his brother, but in a way, everybody understood his story.

In Samdor, we also met several foreign mountaineers. One of them was from Australia and his name was Charles. People said he was a journalist by profession. He interviewed a few of us, and took a photograph of us as well. It was the first time I saw myself in a picture. Before that, I had seen neither a camera nor a photograph of myself.

I had never seen people with blond hair and blue eyes. Seeing them for the first time was a whole new experience. These foreigners were very tall. They Looked very different. I had never seen any foreigners before. I was curious to interact with them, even though I didn't know any words in English. But our group was kind of scared that they might report us either to the Nepali police or to the Chinese police as we were at the border of the two countries. But the moment they showed us the photographs of the Dalai Lama that they were carrying, we felt overjoyed and fully assured to share our experiences with them.

When we ran out of food during the perilous journey, two days seemed like two months, but two days in Samdor passed like two hours. I wished we could stay there forever. But we had to leave the village and walk down the mountain for days.

We were in Nepal, but we still had to walk during nighttime and sleep during daytime. Our guide had lots of stories to tell, and most of them were very scary to listen to.

"At one time, we had a stone fight with a group of Nepali villagers," said the guide.

"Why?" I asked.

"They tried to rob us. There are people on our way to Kathmandu waiting for us to rob us. They are waiting for us like eagles waiting for their prey," said the guide, adding he had travelled this same road several times.

"So, we can make use of our knives!" Tenzin joked.

We sold almost everything in Samdor, but we did not sell our knives. Tibetans in Tibet were fond of knives, and almost everyone had one.

Some had two knives, one for eating meat and one for self-defense. The one for the self-defense was always longer and sharper than the one for eating meat.

Not many people in our group had knives. Tenzin had a big one. I heard that Tenzin had wounded a few Chinese men with that same knife. Tenzin was indeed a scary man when he was angry, but he was our sole hope if we met any robbers on our way to Kathmandu.

For the last few days, it had been raining. It was terrible walking in the rain, but it seemed the rain had kept everyone inside their houses. We were the only ones outside, walking on the road. We felt safe. We hoped it would keep raining until we reached Kathmandu. Our guide said the rain was a blessing.

"His Holiness, the Dalai Lama, is looking upon us," said the guide.

Everyone nodded their heads in agreement. Because of the rain, we were able to walk during daytime, but that night we were walking during the nighttime because we had to cross a police check post.

Our timing was good. We reached the police check post around midnight. The guide and another member of our group went ahead to see if the guards at the check post were still awake or had gone to bed.

We were resting below the main road, which was around five minutes away from the police check post. The two men came back and said that the guards were still awake.

While resting there and waiting for the guards to go to sleep, many of us fell asleep. My mind went back to the past, back to my hometown. I was along with my family. It may sound as weird as it was, but somehow, I knew I was dreaming, but strangely I had control over my dream to keep dreaming and be with my family. I was having a good time with my family, eating coarse *tsampa*, Tibetan barley and drinking Tibetan butter tea. Then, slowly my vision got clouded, and the image of my family faded away. I came back to the reality. I woke up to a flashlight on my face. When I opened my eyes, I saw there were people above on the main road, waving flashlights on our faces. I immediately closed my eyes and pretended that I saw nothing, but my heart was beating so fast. I felt as if my heart was coming out of my mouth. Within seconds, someone from our group shouted, "Run" and everyone tried to get up and run down the hill inside the bushes, but a group of Nepali men came out from the bushes and started yelling at us in Nepali.

These men had sticks and stones in their hands. Apparently, they were with the police. There were around ten Nepali men and ten police officers. We were totally surrounded by them.

They ordered us to come up on the main road, and walk with them to the police station. After getting up on the main road, I followed the presumed leader to the police station, who was directing us to follow him to the station.

"Stick together. Do not go," Tenzin shouted while trying to cocoon Khando under his arms. And all of my group mates tried to form a human chain and stick together. The police officers started hitting us with the butts of their guns, and I could see blood drooling from our mouths, heads and hands. Tenzin curled his fingers forming a fist, and he tried to reach out to his knife. The guide pushed Tenzin's hands away from the knife, and urged everyone to follow the orders of the police officers. Everyone gave in. Within minutes, we were at the police station and we all were thrown inside a room, where we were kept in a corner. The head of the police station with a dark face and a darker mustache curled up towards his nose called us one by one for inspection. They checked all of our bodies including our private parts.

"Oh, it is a woman," said one of the officers as he touched the boobs of a nun.

"Right, it is a nun," another officer touched it again. They all laughed. The nun's tears rolled down on her cheeks. Our group mates lowered their heads down, and kept sobbing. One by one, they snatched our golden chains on our necks and emptied our purses. Without considering us as fellow human beings, they forcefully and disrespectfully confiscated everything that we possessed on our bodies as if they were merely picking fruits from the trees. As they snatched the *Dze*, a precious stone from Khando's neck, Tenzin told them the precious stone was supposed to be offered to the Dalai Lama in memory of their late grandmother. The head of the police station sitting on a chair with his legs crossed, pointed to himself and joked, "I am the Dalai Lama."

The room was dead silent. No one dared to protest. No one even dared to beg. I was neither afraid of the officers nor worried about the confiscation. I had nothing to lose. And I couldn't think of any worse tragedy than the hardship that we had faced during the journey. I begged them not to take the 50 rupees that I had in my pocket. They handed the money back to me.

They kept us at the station for three days. They provided us with a meal once a day. It was not a prison or jail, just a police station.

But we were locked inside the room. No one was allowed to walk out of that room other than me. On the first day, around 10 in the morning, I showed the 50 rupees that I had in my pocket and begged them to let me go out to buy something.

The officers let me go out. I walked out of the station to the small market that was a five minutes walk from the police station. For the whole day, I roamed in the market aimlessly and fearlessly. I feared no one but didn't dare to run away alone. I came back to the station around six in the evening.

The officers paid no attention to me. They simply let me in. My group mates were surprised, but no one scolded me or advised me not to roam alone or run away alone. I was the master of myself and slave of myself. I was on my own. The next day, I did the same thing. Went out into the market. Ate. Had fun, and came back to the station. On the night of the third day, officers escorted us all in a police van and drove us to Kathmandu. We arrived in

Kathmandu the next day around noon. While travelling by van, we saw a few Tibetans walking in the city, and we cried and shouted for help. "Please tell the Tibetan Reception Center that we are being jailed," we shouted, as we knew the Tibetan Reception Center in Kathmandu was responsible for receiving and hosting new arrivals from Tibet. As we shouted for help, and banged on the windows of the bus from inside, many pedestrians outside on the road looked at us in amazement. A grandmother in traditional Tibetan dress with a prayer wheel in her hand stopped walking, waved at us, and shouted back, "Don't worry. I will go and inform them."

We kept screaming for help, and banging on the windows of the bus. The police officers accompanying us in the bus ordered us to keep quiet. They were using us as baits to get money from the Tibetan Reception Center. They warned us if we didn't stay quiet, we would be returned back to Tibet. We kept quiet with tears falling down on our dusty faces into our cracked lips. Tasting the salty, cold tear on our lips, we kept sniffing and staring at each other. We all knew too well what it meant to be handed back to the Chinese police. We would be sentenced to ten years or more.

In Kathmandu, again, we were kept at a police station for three days. On the third day, a man from the Tibetan Reception Center came to bail us out.

The perilous journey was finally over. And we were finally set to be free. But, for me, it also meant that I would not be able to see my family, at least not until I turned into a man; until I finished my studies.

The lump in my throat got only bigger. And my eyes started becoming teary.

7

We were taken out from the police station one by one with a short interview for what felt like an interrogation.

"What is your name?" asked the staff who seemed bored from asking the same questions again and again.

"Tendar," I answered.

"What Tendar? Is it Tenzin Tendar, or Sonam Tendar, or Tendar Tsering?" the officer asked.

"Tendar Tsering," I chose the last one. My real name was Youngdrung Tendar, but I was afraid to reveal my real identity. I feared if I revealed my real name, I would not be admitted into Tibetan Children's Village School. Someone told me that the school was not for Bonpo students, people who were still adamant to replace Tibet's earliest religion, Bon with Buddhism.

After noting my answers, the officer asked, "Are you sure that you want to be a student? Not a monk?"

"No, I don't want to go to a monastery. I want to be a student." I raised my voice, fearing that he was going to send me to a Bonpo monastery.

"OK," the officer said, putting the document in a thick, old file.

I was relieved. With a little smile blossoming on my face, I walked out towards a muddy jeep that I, along with a few other children, was about to take to the Tibetan Reception Center in Kathmandu.

As soon as I reached the Tibetan Reception Center, I was escorted to a clinic that was a mile away from the reception center. A nurse in her early thirties checked my blood pressure, pulse rate and gave me several shots on my left deltoid.

"Brave boy!" the nurse said as I took the

injections without even blinking my eyes.

When I was in Tibet, I used to be scared of injections, but thanks to the perilous journey, now I had become more mature, more responsible and much braver.

Within a few hours of the interrogation and health checkup, I was sent back to the reception center.

The Tibetan Reception Center in Kathmandu was below a small hill, and up on the hill, there was a small Bon monastery. Pointing at the monastery, one of our group mates who knew my real religion said, "That is your monastery, you should make a visit." I knew he was joking and making fun of me, but his joke hit right to the core of my heart.

I was terrified that if the reception officers came to know my real religion, I would not even be allowed to be at the reception center. I really wanted to visit that monastery, but how could I when I couldn't even reveal my real religion? Religion was not one of the categories to be listed while enlisting into the reception center, but I was terrified, like the Tibetan saying goes, "Rabbits worry that the sky might fall down." But I had my reasons to fear, for I had heard about a few minor communal clashes between Bonpo and non-Bonpo people in our hometown in Tibet.

      There were two other Bonpo people in our group: a boy around ten and another, a lady in her late twenties. I didn't know if the lady cared about her religion, but the young boy was also hiding his identity. He revealed his religion to me in secrecy when the man in our group revealed my religion to the group. There were around five hundred people at the reception center. All of them looked pale, and many of them were victims of frostbite. Some had lost legs, some had lost their fingers, and some were suffering from snow blindness. Around thirty more people arrived the day after we arrived. They were also arrested by the Nepali police, and bailed out by the Tibetan Reception Center in Kathmandu. Two of the men in the group were wounded with gunshots, one in his stomach and another on his leg. They said they tried to resist when the

Nepali police arrested them, and that's how the policemen shot them.

However, like us, they were also thankful that the police officers handed them to the Tibetan Reception Center instead of handing them back to the Chinese police in Tibet.

The rooms at the reception center looked like temporary shelters, and the roofing was made out of metal. There were around ten rooms, and each room had dozens of bunk beds. During the day, it was too hot to stay inside the rooms, and during the night, it was almost impossible to have a good sleep as bed bugs were having a feast of our warm blood.

I, along with many others, chose to spend the night outside on the meadow. There were around fifty people sleeping on the meadow, and I could hear all kinds of noise, children having nightmares and shouting their parents' names, frogs croaking, dogs barking and the sound of wind blowing through the trees, and the lady in the corner of the meadow moaning while making love with her new-found boyfriend. I chuckled over the lady's inarticulate, long and low voice of moaning but soon I was occupied by the sound of children crying and shouting their parents' names, making me count the stars and wonder if my parents in Tibet also could see the same stars.

8

I loved our stay in Kathmandu, but I, along with a group of other children and a few elders, was sent to India sooner than we expected. The reception center in Delhi was in the middle of the capital city, and the city was full of people and vehicles alike. It was noisy, crowded and scary. Almost all the people in the city looked like Jackie Chan when it came to jumping in and out of buses. We didn't get to explore the city of Delhi either. We stayed there only for a day. We were set to head to Dharamshala, the seat of the Dalai Lama and the base of Tibetan government in exile. Our bus was on other side of a big main road, which was a ten-minute walk from the reception center. There was an old man trying to escort around forty of us to the bus station through the busy main road, but he lost count of some of us. We were all aliens in the city. Many of us did not know how to cross the main road. We were holding each other's hands, and forming a wave, moving a step back or a step forward depending on the rush of the vehicles on the road.

"Sala, marana chaahata hoon?" an Indian motorcycle rider cursed us as he took a curve away from us.

We stood still in middle of the road, and wondered when we would be crushed to death. I was shivering. I released the hands of two people, and ran ahead without looking to my sides either way. I could hear horns, and the sound of vehicles braking suddenly, and drivers yelling from the windows. Within seconds, I reached the other side of the road. I looked back, and I could see others were still stepping one step forward and one step back. I thought they would all be crushed if they kept holding hands and moving like snails. But they crossed the road within a few minutes. Many of them were sweating.

"Hell, we almost died," breathed Tenzin.

"Drivers are also people, we don't have to be scared," I said.

"Yeah, right, look at your pants," Tenzin laughed.

I looked down, and saw I had peed in my pants. I kept silent, and walked ahead.

Finally, we reached the bus station, and we were reunited with the rest of our group mates. It was a relief. The old man who was supposed to escort us to the bus station was waiting for us there, and the moment he saw us, he yelled at us to quicken our steps. We ran and jumped in the bus. It was an old bus with almost all the seats torn apart. Within minutes, the bus started moving. I sat down next to an old woman, and slept.

9

Dharamshala was in a hilly area, and we reached there early in the morning. It was foggy, cold, and many of the houses resembled those of Tibetans with colorful Buddhist prayer flags hanging on the roofs of their houses. I felt a sense of joy and welcoming and home. The bus stopped in the middle of the town, and we had to walk for five minutes down to the reception center. The road was a little congested with shops and booths on both sides. We fought our way to the reception center through a sea of Tibetans and Indians, cows and dogs, where everyone seemed to call the town their home.

Once we reached the reception center, we were given a few food tokens and a pair of blankets and they directed us to sleep in a big hall. They had already served the breakfast, and lunch was several hours away.

My stomach was growling. I went away to a restaurant in the market.

As soon as I entered the restaurant, a waitress in her early 20s came to me with a menu in her hand. The menu was in English, and I could read only the price.

"You have momo?" I asked if the restaurant sold dumpling.

"Yes," replied the waitress.

"How much?"

"15 Rupees per plate."

"You provide soup with momo?"

"Yes,"

"How much for the soup?"

"Soup is free,"

"Ok,"

I flipped the menu a few times, knowing I couldn't order momo as I had only ten Rupees in my pocket.

"You have chowmein?" I asked.

"Yes,"

"How much?"

"Same price,"

"Ok,"
I couldn't ask any more questions. I remained Silent for a second and said, "Thank you." It was an awkward moment. The waitress also went away saying, "Let me know when you are ready."

"Ok," I replied humbly.
I stayed in the restaurant for a few more minutes, flipping the menu, and then asked, "Can I have just the soup?"

"Soup comes only with the momo," replied the waitress with a chuckle.

The man who was at the counter said something to the waitress, and the waitress shortly gave me a plate of momo, and a bowl of soup.

"Only soup please," I said.

"It is ok. It is free," shouted the man from the desk while walking towards me.

"Thank you," I said.

The man asked if he could sit next to me at the same table. I said, 'sure.'
He never introduced himself to me, but he was

full of questions. The man asked me about my journey and about my hometown in Tibet. He didn't seem moved by my story, but he looked glad to hear about Tibet. I ate the momo and drank the soup in minutes. He asked me if I wanted more. I replied, 'No.' The man wished me all the best, and gave me 100 Rupees. I was in heaven. My face started blossoming with a smile. I thanked the man, and walked down to the reception center with my hand on the money in my pocket, jumping and singing, and kicking empty cans on the street.

Once I reached the reception center, everybody was in line outside the reception office. I joined in the queue, and we were again asked the same questions; what was your name, where were you going and how old were you? I gave them the same answers; Tendar Tsering, 12 and going to school.

"Age 12?" asked the officer.

"Yes," I replied.

"Here in the document, your age is noted as 11?" asked the officer.

"Ok. I am 11 years old," I replied.

"11 or 12?" asked the officer while frowning his eyebrows. He had more eyebrows than hair on his head.

"11," I said, trying not to glance at his hairless head.

His eyes scanning me from my head to toe, he noted my age, and I became younger by one year.

The Tibetan Reception Center in Dharamshala was no different from the reception center in Kathmandu and Delhi, but at least, there were fewer bedbugs. However, I constantly had to scratch my body and shrug my shoulders as I could feel lice were moving from one part to another on my back, on my legs and even on my thing in between my thighs.

The whole day, I sat on my bed and looked around to make sure no one was looking at me scratch myself. Everybody was staying together in one big hall. There were around 80 beds.

I could see everyone in the room, as it was a big open hall. People were coming in, people were going out. Some were crying, some were in shock, and some were in joy after meeting their loved ones after decades of separation.

I wished someone would come in with a bunch of gifts and be introduced to me as one of my father's old friends or someone who hailed from my hometown. But it was all in vain. No one came. I was tired of daydreaming, and went to bed, hoping someone would come to see me the next day.

10

I was woken up by the usual irritating and annoying sound of our guide shouting, "Today we are going to see the Dalai Lama." If he didn't kick or pull away my blanket, I would not be able to differentiate between his voice and a frog's croaking sound. I hated his voice. Everybody hated his voice. But that morning, he delivered the news that everyone had been waiting for. Smiles started blossoming on the faces of everyone in the hall. Some elders sat back and closed their eyes, letting the joyful news soak into their bones and savor the moment.

The guide was smiling and jumping in joy, and he threw a towel, a small packet of toothpaste and a toothbrush to me.
"Do you know how to brush your teeth?" he laughed. It was hard to say if he was trying to make fun of me, or he was flying in joy.
 "I know," I smiled. I rarely smiled but I smiled

even to the man that I loathed the most.

Our guide knew that many people in Tibet didn't brush their teeth, even for years. When I was in Tibet, I also hadn't brushed my teeth once. People in my hometown, hardly ever washed their face either. On special occasions, we would wash our face with walnuts. We would grind walnuts with our teeth, and pour the mixture out on our palms, and rub it on our face. It would look filthy but in a place where the temperature was often below zero degrees, that had been a tradition for centuries.

One of my uncles used to live in a city, and whenever he came home, he would brush his teeth and wash his face with water instead of walnuts. And I was going to be like my uncle. I took the toothbrush, rubbed the toothpaste on it, and went out to the water tap. I washed my face and brushed my teeth. I felt very refreshed. I rushed back to my room and grabbed my bowl, and the food token and went to the kitchen for breakfast.

There was a long line of people, and I had

to wait for fifteen minutes with the bowel in my right hand, and the food token in my left hand. They served beef noodle soup, and I was overjoyed to know that meat was available in India. It was the first time for me to eat meat since I had arrived in the country. I thought meat was not available in India as someone told me India was a land of vegetarians. And on the other day, I had been hoping for a meat momo but the restaurant offered me a vegetarian momo.

After breakfast, we went to the Dalai Lama's residence. It was a twenty-minute walk from the reception center. The Dalai Lama's residence in India didn't look like his residence in Tibet. But it was a quiet, peaceful residence with lots of flowers in the backyard. The spiritual leader's residence was highly guarded. Security officers checked our bodies, our bags and everything that we possessed. Then, an old officer escorted us to a small room, and we waited. After ten minutes, a monk in his late 50s came in from another door. All eyes gazed at the monk. I thought he was the Dalai Lama but I was wrong. We kept waiting for around five more minutes. The room was so quiet. No one was speaking. No one was moving one's body or eyes. Dead silence. We were impatiently sitting in the room and waiting for the Dalai Lama. A few of elders in our group came to India to merely meet the Dalai Lama. They were literarily ready to even sacrifice their lives in order to see the spiritual leader in person. So, an audience with the spiritual leader meant everything to them.

I looked around, both Tenzin and the guide were praying under their breaths. They were motionless except their lips and their wrinkles on their foreheads, constantly moving up and down as if they were about to follow the suit of Lord Buddha's enlightenment. I slowly tapped on Tenzin's elbow and asked him, "What's up?" He signaled me to keep quiet. Then his head bending towards mine, he said, "From today onwards, you are being offered to the Dalai Lama. You are a son of the Dalai Lama.

Behave yourself."

Suddenly, a monk came in, and all the people in the room started sobbing. He was the Dalai Lama. Before sitting down on his throne, he asked someone in the front row,

"How was your journey?"

The man couldn't utter a word. He just kept bending down his head and kept crying. The whole room was crying. I looked at Khando, she was not crying. I moved my eyes around, and looked at Khando again. She was in awe. I was also in shock. We winked at each other, questioning why all the people in the room were crying.

      The Dalai Lama patted and rubbed the man's head gently, looked at the audience, and sat down. He kept silent for a second, then, uttered a few prayers under his breath with his hands joined together and placed under his chin, and then he started speaking. He spoke for twenty minutes. He urged the audience to be calm and happy. At the end, the Dalai Lama stood up, and we all walked towards him one by one to get his blessing before leaving the room.

"Where are you from?" the Dalai Lama asked me.

"Tsawa Rongpa," I replied.

"Khangtruk, khangtruk," he rubbed my head in a way as if he knew me for a long time, and I felt loved.

We came out of the Dalai Lama's residence, and everyone looked so happy. I asked Khando, "What is Khangtruk?"

"I don't know," she answered.

I asked the guide the same question, and he said, "Khangtruk means bad boy."

I felt terrible. I told myself *that makes sense. I am a bad boy, that's why, my parents sent me away.* That thought hit right to the core of my heart. I almost cried. But then, Khando's father jumped in the conversation, and said, "You are from Khang, north eastern side of Tibet, and children from there are called Khangtruk."

The guide laughed. He again made fun of me. I was a little relieved, but a part of my mind still reminded me that I was a bad body, because

I shouted on the mountains, and killed a frog by blowing air into it's anus with the help of a straw and knocked off with a stone. I regretted what I did then, but the memory of mingling with my friends and hunting frogs brought tears to my eyes.

11

After four days in Dharamshala, I was sent to a Tibetan Children's Village School in India. The school was several miles away from the reception center.

There were lots of children like myself. Some were as young as four years old but most of them were around seven to fifteen years old.

When I reached the school, students encircled me as if I were an animal in a zoo. All of them looked curious. They stopped playing. With balls and kites in their hands, they stood still and murmured to each other. Their eyes wide open and excitedly asking me from which part of Tibet I came from, I could understand they were homesick. All of them were hoping to get a piece of news about their families in Tibet from me.

"They are also like you. They all have come from Tibet and they don't have any parents or relatives here." A lady in her forties took my hand in hers asking me to call her "home mother." I walked with her to a house with a little garden in front of the house. Outside the house, by the door, it was written *Home Number One*.

The lady introduced me to the rest of the children at the house and urged them to consider me as one of their own family members. They all looked fresh, energetic and happy. They didn't look like orphans, or semi-orphans, or unwanted and discarded children.

"This is going to be your home away from home, and they all are your brothers and sisters," said the lady as if she was my newly found mother.

My mouth wide open, in awe and disbelief, I nodded my head telling myself *I am a student now and I am at my home away from home.*

12

Several months after I got admitted into the school, our school director came to our home, and asked about my journey. I told him that our journey took one month and twenty-three days. He selected me for an interview with a group of journalists in Dharamshala. He had selected four more children from other homes in the school, and the next day, he took five of us to Dharamshala.

    To my surprise, the Australian journalist who I met in Samdor was also there along with two other journalists. The journalist recognized me and I recognized him. They interviewed us for half an hour. We thought that they would give us some gifts, but they didn't give us anything. They gave us their business cards, which we threw in the dustbin as we walked out of the restaurant where we met them.

A few years later, our school secretary informed me that I had four sponsors to whom I had to write thank you letters, Christmas and New Year's cards.

Every month, my sponsors would pay my school fee. Every month, each sponsor would pay $40 as my school fee. So, technically, they were paying $160 per month. I was lucky among unlucky ones. Some of the students at the school didn't have a single sponsor, so, our school would substitute some of my school fees for those who didn't have any sponsor.

Some students built relationships with their sponsors, but for many, their sponsors were just their sponsors, nothing more, nothing less, other than feeling grateful to the sponsors. Very often, our school sponsor secretary would erase our sponsors' addresses in the letters, and every letter, or card was supposed to go through the school sponsor secretary only. No private contacts at all. It was a rule. But I was able to build a private contact with two of my sponsors, who helped me throughout my studies. I even built a family like relationship with one of the sponsors— a German couple, but later, I realized it was just a one-sided relationship. I was meant to be helped, but not to be loved. But they would always be in my heart, and I would always follow their steps to help those who were in need of help. That was my way of paying for what I had received.

My sponsors were my angels, and I had written hundreds of letters, thanking them for their help, but I had never thanked the person who was the reason behind all the help that I enjoyed throughout my studies.

Probably, it was the Australian journalist, who brought me all the luck. One of my sponsors with whom I was able to build a connection, in private later told me that she saw me in the news, and decided to sponsor me. I wished I hadn't torn the Australian journalist's business card and dumped into the dustbin. So that I could at least write him a thank you letter.

13

There were three types of students in our school. Some were bookworms and they were usually bad in sports and music but had good manners and they were usually the teachers' favorite students. Then there was another group of students who were naughty and bad in studies but good at sports, or music and they were the super stars among the students. And there were a few others who were well mannered but bad in all sports, or music and studies. They were the ones who had nothing when they graduated from the school. I had a few friends here and there but most of my friends belonged to the first group, and so did I.

"If anyone wants to find Tendar Tsering, one doesn't have to look far, one can directly go to the library or his room." My friends used to tell one another. They were right. I was more insider than outsider, and during the day, I spent most of my time either in the library or on my bed reading anything that came across me.

At night, it was our school's rule to switch off the room lights by ten o' clock, and I used to read in the toilet. It was stinky at times but very quiet and peaceful. If someone came to use the toilet, I had to step out until the person was done.

If I found an interesting book, I wouldn't put it down until I finished it. Sometimes, I would even read while walking from home to class, or class to home. Since I couldn't afford to go and experience the real world, books were the only ways that I could see and experience the world. I would read around ten books in a month, and reading books written by children like Anne Frank inspired me to become a writer.

I started keeping a diary, and I thought that I had the materials to write a good memoir. I had seen writers and filmmakers who came to our school, spent a week or two, and wrote books or made documentary films about us.

Sometimes, I read storybooks even on the day of school exams and joked around among our friends by saying, "I study for life, not for exam." But the fact was, I also studied for exams. Doing well in exams was the only way that I could garner our teachers' appreciation. If one did poorly in the exams, consequences were always harsh that could even end one's life, or career. Being a shy student, I could never imagine myself being pointed out in front of all the students to be warned, or whipped, or embarrassed.

Those who did well in exams were always overvalued, over appreciated and the rest were always under valued. Exams were everything in India. Exams were gateways to get into colleges, jobs thereafter and even to enter into the next grade level, exams were the only sole deciding factors. Exam related suicide was common in the country. Every year, thousands of students in the country were said to end their lives because they didn't do well in their exams.

I had not personally seen anyone end

their lives in our school because of the exams, but I had seen students running away, or dropping out of school and roaming in the streets because they didn't do well in their exams. In silence, I wished the schools could value and empower the students in other ways as well, not just based on exams. For example, one of my friends was well versed in Tibetan language and he was a great writer. I loved his writings, and he was a great storyteller as well. Students would sit around him during nighttime, and listen to his stories.

He would tell stories by mimicry, sound, action, and we felt as if we were watching a movie. During our tenth grade, he did not do well in his math exam, and had to drop out of school. Otherwise, he was sure to become a great writer, or a scholar in Tibetan language.

14

When summer began, so did my love and hate relationship with the season. I loved the beautiful, warm weather but hated the long days. Long days with limited meals, I often felt there was nothing more than water in my stomach. I could hear my stomach growling, and I even could feel water zigzagging down my intestines.

    I kept rubbing my lips together to swallow down as much saliva as possible. During meals, I ate in a hurry and that helped to make my stomach feel full at least for a moment. Otherwise, meals were not only limited, but little in quantity as well. The worst part was we didn't know how to walk, we often ran and that for sure, consumed most of our energy, and made us in need of more food to eat.

    There were co-curricular activities

where we had to participate in athletics, marathons and basketball, football and volleyball matches. After school, we had to run for miles up to the Indian market through the tea plants.
I would hide myself inside the tea plant bushes and read books. And sometimes, we had to wake up and run for miles around five in the morning. I would again hide myself under a school office building and read books with the help of a streetlight. When it was dawn, I would join the rest of the students as they would return back to the school playground, and act as if I had been running all along with them.

Our school schedule was often long and school curriculums were never ending. School life was tiring and boring most of the time. I hated my classes and seeing the same faces for years. School clinic was the place where almost every student wanted to stay a night or two.

Some students pretended to be sick in order to get leave from the classes. A few students were very good at faking and getting sick leaves.

I hated the medicines, but school clinic was such a heaven to me. If anyone fell sick and was able to stay at the clinic, every morning, we would get to eat a banana and a cup of milk besides getting to miss the classes.

I once pretended to be sick and went to the school dispensary, but all in vain.
I tried to look sick with a sad mood on my face and coughing but somehow, the nurse said, "you don't look sick."

"I am sick. I am having high fever as well," I insisted.
The nurse put a thermometer in my mouth, and she left the room. I took out the thermometer and rinsed it with hot water and put it back in my mouth. The nurse came back, and she was shocked. It was way over normal temperature. But the nurse didn't believe it. She touched her hand on my hand, and said, "Strange, I don't feel any temperature."

She put the thermometer back in my mouth, and waited for a few minutes, and took out.

"You are fine. You don't have any fever," said the nurse.
She gave me a few medicines and didn't give me a sick leave.

"Nurse, I am really not feeling well, please give me a sick leave," I begged.

"There, you go, you just want the sick leave." She even took the medicines back from me and warned me if I tried to fake again, she would report me to the school headmaster.

I went to the class, regretting, and knowing I shouldn't have faked being sick in the first place.

But then, there was a small child, around nine years old, and at that time, I was sixteen, and I noticed he was often on sick leave, and enjoying his off time from the classes.

I knew he was lying because he didn't look sick and played with us whenever we held a basketball match or soccer match.
"How do you manage to get a sick leave?" I asked.

"Onion,"

"How?"

"Keep onion under your arm for a few minutes, and your temperature will go up," he said.

I was overjoyed, and thought I had mastered the trick of cheating and getting a sick leave but when I was planning to take a sick leave, someone told me that there was a line of students outside the school dispensary the other day, and the school nurse came to know all of them had used the "onion method."

Some students would rub mud on their eyes, and that would allow them to stay at the school clinic for a day or two. I didn't dare do that because their eyes really looked red and terrible.

My father once told me that he would be praying to Lord Buddha to keep me safe and healthy. I also prayed to Lord Buddha but for a different reason. For I knew my father had prayed to keep me healthy, I even tried to negotiate with Lord Buddha.

"Lord, please don't listen to my father at

least once, and make me sick for a few days. If you grant me my wish, I will donate Rupee 5000 to a monastery when I grow up. I mean Rupee 500." I prayed, but all in vain.

Buddha was always on my father's side, and that made sense as my father had been praying for his whole life.

15

I was neither the tallest nor the shortest student in our school. But I was one of the thinnest students. I was as skinny as a skeleton. Some would call me skeleton, and others would call me giraffe, or *gochen*, meaning big head. I was so thin that it made my head seem bigger and neck seem longer. I looked like a scarecrow. If I stood for sometime in the sun during summer, my hands and arms would become sweaty and veins would bulge out. I would always try to cover my arms and hands, as they were nothing but skeletons with veins.

I felt docile. Out casted. Often left out and alone. I would walk with my head and chin digging into my chest, and I shivered while walking in public.

Whenever there was a class picnic, or

camping trip, our whole class would shout in joy, but I would often cry in silence.

Most of my classmates had relatives in India, and their economic conditions were relatively better than mine. They knew my economic condition and whenever the students formed groups during the picnics, or camping trips, none of them would include me.
It was always the class teacher who would ask around if anyone would like to include me in their group. Some kind and mature students would say, "Tendar can join our group." I was relieved, but I was again left not knowing whether to cry or laugh. I was happy that a group was at least going to include me but at the same time, I could hear pitiful murmurs, "Nyin ji, look at Tendar."

And my classmates would always spare me from collecting funds for the class picnic, or camping trip. I felt thankful to them but at the same time, I felt terrible, I felt worse. Being a teenager, I was ashamed of myself. Sometimes, I would try to excuse myself from the picnic, or camping trip.

Our class teacher would excuse me from joining the class picnic, or camping trip, but my whole classmates knew I was ashamed to join them, because I was unable to pay my due amount for the picnic, or camping trip.

"I would pay for Tendar." Sometimes someone in the class would surprise me by paying for the picnic or camping trip on my behalf.

"No, I am not going. I am not feeling well," I would say.

"Tendar becomes sick whenever we plan for a picnic." Sometimes, some freaky, innocent students in the class would laugh at me and make fun of my condition.

My face became red. My eyes became teary. My voice shivering, I would try to convince them that I was really not feeling well.

"Quiet, quiet, Tendar is not feeling well. So, let him stay back," our class teacher would shout.

I was relieved. And while they were enjoying their camping trip in the neighboring mountains, I would be wetting my bed with my tears of loneliness, homesickness and sadness.

I had always felt docile. Weak. Powerless. Retarded. The best thing about being lonely and aloof was that I started studying more. Being good in studies was my only strength. So, I kept studying, and it worked. I started getting noticed, appreciated and acknowledged for my talent in writing, both in Tibetan and English.

I started getting friends of all kinds. Some would come for help to give them Tibetan tuition, and some would seek help to interpret passages or poetry in English. In return, they would give me pencils or pens that I could use during my exams. They would also lend me their clothes during the New Year celebrations, so I didn't have to wear worn out socks and worn out shoes. I hated walking with my worn out shoes, as my shoes would make a lub dub sound with my toes often peeping out of my shoes. I would sometimes try to tie my shoes around my feet in order to escape myself from making the lub dub sound.

When it rained, I would wrap plastic bags around my feet and wear my worn-out shoes to protect my feet from being soaked.

Most of the students hated the school uniforms, and they would go gala when we could wear our own clothes. But, for me, it was other way around.

Every year, our school would provide us with a pair of shoes, socks, shirts and pants. We would mark our school uniforms with our names on them, or sometimes, we would tear our shirts or pants to make them recognizable.

Since all uniforms were alike, other than the different sizes, small, medium and large, every morning, there would be a quarrel over the uniforms. Every night, I would keep my uniforms under my pillow. In that way, I didn't have to fight for my uniform when I wake up. I would polish my shoes with my black ink, and it would keep the shoes shinning for a day or two. Neat and tidy was what we were supposed to look throughout the day, but they would rarely provide us soaps to wash our faces or oil to put on our hair. I would steal cooking oil from the kitchen and use it on my hair, and flies often danced over my head because of the cooking oil.

Sometimes, I would wash my hair with soap, and never rinse the soap bubbles from my hair. In that way, I could keep my hair in any direction that I wanted to keep— Beckham hairstyle or Ricky Martin hairstyle.

16

It had been eight years since I joined the Tibetan Children's Village School and I would be graduating from the school in less than two years, but it felt like I had joined the school a year ago.

Now the school had truly become my home away from home, and everyone here knew me as Tendar Tsering. Not long after joining this school, I learned that no one really cared what my religion was, but I was still living in a hidden world. When I arrived at the school, I became a new person. I had a new religion. I was a Buddhist. But I was also a Bonpo for I saw no difference between the two. I spoke a few languages, and I loved writing. I wrote Christmas letters to sponsors on behalf of my friends at our school and that had become my annual routine. Every year, I would write dozens of Christmas letters, and I would get lots of gifts once my friends would receive Christmas gifts from their sponsors.

We were probably the only people in this world who never celebrated Christmas but always eagerly waited for the day. During Christmas, we would get lots of gifts from our sponsors in the west.

Many of our sponsors were liberals who would skip going out to dinners in order to sponsor us by paying our school fees and sending us gifts on special occasions like Christmas and New Year. Apart from writing Christmas letters and New Year's cards for my friends, I also loved writing. So far, I had written more than twenty diaries. All were unread except by myself. I didn't think that my world would turn upside down if anyone happened to read my diaries, but I didn't want anyone to read them. As writing had become my ultimate passion, so my diaries had become my ultimate soul mate with whom I could share anything that came to my mind.

Khando once asked me, "What do you write in your diary book?" She was curious as she hated writing and believed, "Writing means torture to the mind."

"Routine stuff," I said.

"Anything that comes to my mind," I added.

"Everything? Anything?" asked Khando.

Khando was the only person I had known since I had joined the school. We were too small back then, but I guess my heart was kind of locked into hers since the day that she gave me a chocolate cookie and asked me to be her friend while we were on our way to India from Tibet. She was ten and I was twelve then. Both of us had grown up and we had been friends for around eight years.

"Yes, Tendar loves noting down how much he eats and how much he shits," Dawa, another friend of mine jumped in, interrupting the conversation, and all of my friends at the boarding school started laughing. I too, started laughing. That was how we cherished our days at the school, laughing over silly jokes.

Khando's father was a cook at our school, and Dawa's brother was a teacher at our school. I envied them a lot. In fact, all of my friends at the boarding school had either relatives or family members in India with whom they could depend on, or share their feelings whenever they needed them.

So, if I told them that diary writing meant everything to me, they wouldn't even understand what I meant by that. So, answering 'anything' was probably more reasonable than answering 'everything.'

My answers were usually just two words when it came to something that I didn't feel like talking much about, and my friends had mastered when to stop bombarding me with questions.

Since the school was on vacation, most of the students had already gone for the two-month winter holiday. Those who were left back in the school were those from Tibet who had nowhere to go. Like every year, that year too, my tears burst out like boiling water falling out of a hot pot making me tremble. I often ran into the nearby forest and shouted out my mom's name. I unceasingly looked up into the sky and when I saw birds flying in the sky, I wished I could borrow their wings, so I could fly back to my hometown at least once. I knew my mom wouldn't hear my scream nor could I borrow the birds' wings but merely being in the forest helped me to soothe myself at least for the moment.

One year after another, gradually, I stopped running into the forest. I stopped seeing the birds in the forest. My eyes had become tearless. I was becoming matured faster than the others who were my same age. I looked older than my age. I even behaved like a fully-grown up man. But there were a few occasions that never let me stop missing my family. One was when the students returned from holiday with lots of candies, and chocolates. The other occasion that used to sadden me the most as a child was when my schoolmates left for their holidays. Most of my classmates eagerly waited for the winter holiday, as that was the only time that they could spend time with their family. But I hated winter holidays. It was cold and most of the time, very windy. During winter, the school looked deserted with only a few children left in the school. I liked summer time more. Our school was located in a remote, peaceful area surrounded by tea trees and trees of all kinds. During summer, everything was so green with the green tea trees surrounding the school and even our school uniform was green in color. But then there were a few things that made me hate the summer as well, long days with short nights was one of them.

During summer, we had to wake up at five in the morning. I hated to wake up that early. Then, the school would make us sleep for two hours in the afternoon. I hated taking naps.

Long days were like jail time to us when we had to take a nap in the middle of the day. During long days, very often, our stomachs used to growl for more food but there were only three limited meal times in a day; breakfast in morning, lunch in middle of the day and dinner in the evening. One slice of bread with a cup of sweet tea for breakfast, rice and dal for lunch, and one and half tiny piece of steamed bread with a bowl of vegetables for dinner. Many children at the boarding school went hungry as they exchanged their food with candies. At one time, I also got to skip my breakfast because the day before, I had already sold my breakfast to one of my friends in exchange for licking his candy three times.

When I was in middle school, a few of my friends and I requested the director of our school to increase the quantity and quality of our meals. For whatever reason, our director got so angry and he even drove his old jeep to our home and told us that he was going to return us back to Tibet. We were so scared because if he returned us back to Tibet, we would be jailed for years, even decades.

"We are surviving on donations from the

west. We have enough money to feed you even if we feed you all with meat meals everyday, but we have to think for the long term," the director started lecturing us.

After one and a half hours of lecturing, the director asked us if we wanted to ask any questions. As usual, none of us asked any questions. At such lectures or meetings, we hardly raised our voice. That was because we were so often taught to be humble, respectful and obedient.

Like most of my schoolmates, I too loved our school and our school was our home away from home, but punishment and beating were part of the school tradition. The more the teacher was strict and the more the teacher punished the students, that teacher was hailed as sincere, dedicated and sometimes patriotic as well. But in my later years there, things were changing for the better. The founder of our school, who is the sister of His Holiness the Dalai Lama banned the teachers from beating the students. Many teachers protested against the ban. Some teachers even resigned in protest against the new rule. Since then, beating became illegal in our school. If a teacher was reported beating students, then, the teacher's salary would be reduced, or at worst, the teacher could be fired from the school.

One day, as we were playing basketball, our Tibetan language teacher stopped us and scolded us for wearing our pants low on our waist and showing our underwear. He scolded us and he threatened us, but didn't dare to raise a hand on us. He let us go after two or three minutes of lecture. The moment he let us go, one of our classmates ran a little ahead and turned back and shouted "sir" while making a round circle in the air with his middle finger. The teacher looked disappointed rather than angry. He didn't add a word, went away nodding his head in dismay.

17

Our Tibetan New Year was coming up. It was just twenty days away. That year, the Tibetan New Year and Chinese New Year were said to be on the same day according to the Tibetan calendar.

"Even our calendar wants us to be part of China," said Khando.

"It is destined," I added.

"I disagree," said Dawa. When it came to topics such as religion or the Tibet-China issue, all of my friends shared similar ideologies except Dawa who believed Tibet and China were never meant to be together.

As usual, Dawa got a little angered by our conversation and he started yelling at us. We debated for around fifteen minutes. Dawa got more angry, and walked out to get some fresh air and came back.

As Dawa came in, Khando asked him, "You know that even His Holiness the Dalai Lama wants us to be part of China?"

"Don't use the Dalai Lama card," said Dawa.

"If you bring the Dalai Lama into our debate, I have nothing to say," added Dawa.

Everyone in the school knew about Dawa's family history. His father was one of the ex-Tibetan soldiers who helped the Dalai Lama escape from Tibet to India in 1959.
We ended the debate as it was getting heated. We changed our topic to the New Year.

We all agreed that there was no excitement in celebrating the New Year.

I used to love the New Year celebrations when I was with my family in Tibet but since I departed from my family, I hated such celebrations as they made me homesick. So was the case with many of my schoolmates. Every year on New Year's day, I used to make a phone call to my family in Tibet.

Most of the time the line was not reachable. If I was able to reach them, it was like a crying day. We all cried. We didn't talk much. There was no point of talking because we all lied. We lied all the time. I lied to my parents about myself, and I knew they would do the same. None of us wanted to sadden each other. We never shared bad news.

We always shared good news. All was well. That year, I did not want to call them on the Tibetan New Year day because I didn't want to make them cry on the first day of the New Year, but if I didn't call them, they would get worried about me. So, I decided to call them a few days ahead of the New Year to inform them that I would not be calling them on New Year's Day.

18

After more than two hours of waiting in line, I finally got my turn to use the phone. There was only one phone booth in our school. The phone booth was always in use; students, staff and local Indians always jammed the booth waiting for their turn to use the phone. Calling Tibet was very expensive. 27 Rupees per minute. Many of my friends would call their parents to tell them to call back. I wished I could do that as well but my family lived in a remote area and to make a phone call to me, they had to drive for a day or two.

We spoke for fifteen minutes over the phone. Exactly fifteen minutes. I couldn't afford to speak more than that. I had only fifteen dollars, earned from writing Christmas and New Year's cards for my friends. As usual, we never uttered a word about the Dalai Lama nor spoke anything about the ongoing Tibet-China issue. We merely spoke about ourselves. Unlike before, that time my family shared with me bad news that made me blue for days.

"Can I speak to grandpa?" I asked my mom over the phone.

"He is not here," said my mother.

"Where did he go?" I asked without any second thought.

"Gone," said my mom.

"Gone?" I asked as my eyes already started welling up with tears.

"It has been two years since he passed away," said my mom, consoling me and urging me to come and see them as soon as possible.

My tears rolled down my cheeks like water from a dam. I looked up and looked down trying to console myself. With a long breath, I said, "Two more years, mom."

For years, my mom had been begging me to return home and for years, I had been giving her the same reply, "Two more years."

I guess it was my family's way of trying to reduce my loneliness by keeping secrecy about the passing away of my loved ones and sharing the sad news with me only after years had gone by.

I would be eighteen the next year and would be graduating from the school soon. It had been more than eight years since I had seen my family in Tibet and in these years, a lot of people in my town had passed away including some of my dear and near ones.

I really wanted to take a gap year from my studies and return home to see my family but I was scared. Two of my schoolmates went back to Tibet and they were reportedly caught by the Chinese police at the border, and sentenced to six years each. I was a coward when it came to Chinese police. I would probably shiver even at the glance of Chinese soldiers in their uniform.

My friend, Khando was more courageous and more reasonable. She believed that we were little over brainwashed by our school teachers.

"We don't have to fear the Chinese police unless we really are involved in political activities. They are also human beings," Khando often encouraged me to return home.

"Yeah," I answered.

Deep down in my heart, I always knew that I would never ever return home. I was so scared to return home. As long as we were in India, we were fated to be jailed if we returned to Tibet.

The desire to return home and the fear of being caught and jailed tore me apart.

19

Making a phone call to my family in Tibet was so expensive. I would be able to call them only once in awhile, but things were changing in last few years. It was much cheaper than before, and I could call my family quite often. But I always knew that the Beijing government could tap our conversations. I never spoke about politics. If my siblings asked me about politics, I would always appreciate the Beijing government.

"People are saying China is becoming the most powerful country in the world. Is it true?" my brother was full of questions. Sometimes, I would call him a question bank.

"Yes, that is true. These days, China is becoming more powerful than the United States," I would answer.

No matter how much we hated the fact that China occupied our country, but my brother was always glad to hear that China was becoming powerful. Sadly, I could clearly see that my fake appreciation of Beijing government in fact turning my brother into a communist.

My father was a wise man. He knew when I was lying. He was sensitive. He was a little overcautious. My mother was worse. She had a chicken heart. She was always scared of speaking with me. I knew both of my parents were desperate to see me, and they were missing me as much as I missed them, but sometimes, when they were too concerned about their safety, that would often make me wonder if I was their son.

It was always my younger brother, with whom, I would speak for hours, but I suddenly lost his contact for months. Then, one day, I was able to reach him. We spoke for hours. He told me that all of our family members were in good health and they were just busy as *Yagtsagumpo* season was coming up where the entire town would become deserted, as everyone would be on the mountains in search of *Yagtsagumgo*.

Then, the next day, he told me some Chinese officials came to our house and they wanted me to give them call. He gave me their phone number.

I didn't call. I told my brother that the phone number was not working. He gave me another number. I told him the phone line was not reachable. He later insisted me to call them as soon as possible. I didn't call. One day from nowhere, I got a call from an unknown number.

"*Tashi Delek*, how are you? I am the one that your brother was talking about," a man on the other side of the phone introduced himself as one of the public security officers from my hometown in Tibet. He was speaking in Tibetan language. He was a Tibetan. He got a thick Khampa accent, but I could understand him. I got goose bumps. I was left without any words. Then, I said, *"Kyapa Tashi Delek,"* of course, only under my breath. After cursing the official in my mind momentarily, replied, "*Tashi Delek*, I am good. How are you?"

"Good, good," the officer said.

"Good," I repeated.

"The reason that I am contacting you is that we are hoping if you can give your heart to our 'motherland' even though you live outside the country," the official said.

I laughed. Then, I asked myself, "which country this bastard was referring to—Tibet or China?" But of course, I knew he was referring to China. Again, I picked up my phone and replied, "I don't think that I can do anything for the 'mother land'."

"Yes, you can do a lot," he said.

"You don't have to do much. You have to advise other Tibetans in your area not to protest against the Beijing government," he added.

"Honestly, I never spoke about politics with my family in Tibet, and even if I spoke, I would say only good things about China," I said.

"That is good. You have to advise other Tibetans in your area also," he said.

"I don't think that I can do that, but I won't encourage my family in Tibet to involve in any anti-China movement," I said.

"Okay," the officer said.

"What are you doing there?"

"I am a student?"

"What are you studying?"

"I am intending to become a medical doctor," I lied.

"Okay. If you need any financial help, let us know and we can help you."

"No, I am okay. I don't need any help."

"Okay, if you need any help in the future, contact us."

"Okay," I said.

"Okay," the officer ended the call. I was much relieved, but I couldn't help thinking about the safety of my family.

After a few days, I again lost contact with my brother for weeks.

I tried to contact my friends and other family members and relatives in Tibet, but I could reach anyone of them.

Then, one day, I was able to contact a friend in my hometown. From him, I came to know that my brother had been arrested by the Chinese officials and interrogated for weeks. He said that the entire town was under house arrest for a month.

"Officials come and check our cell phones at any day, so please don't contact me from today onwards," he said. His voice was shaking.

"Okay," I said.

"I am sorry about that," he said.

"It is okay," I said.

We ended our conversation. I went out into a nearby forest and lay down, looking up into the wide sky. My thoughts again led me to the land of blaming on myself, "I was born to be a troublemaker, I am a trouble maker."

I closed my eyes and I opened my eyes again. I looked up into the sky. This time, the sun was too
bright that I couldn't look up anymore. The sky was the only thing familiar to me and been with me since I was born, but this time, I felt even the sun in the sky was ignoring me. I lay there for some time, and then came back to my room. I shared the news with some of my friends and they advised me not to contact my family in

Tibet.

"I am sure the last thing that you want to do is to put your family in jail. So just stop contacting your family," one of my friends advised me.

A part of myself was saying, "Yes, move on. It is high time for you to move on. Just forget about the past, let your family live in peace and move on with your life."

But another part of myself was saying, "No, there is no meaning in life if I can't contact with my family in Tibet."

I was divided into two. A part of myself was struck with the past and a part of myself was trying to move on and live a normal life.

20

Winter holiday was over. School was set to resume. All students had returned from the holiday. All the locker rooms were full of edibles and toys. I didn't feel sad or jealous of the gifts of toys and edibles that the students got from their holiday. Instead, I felt content, proud and happy knowing that I didn't waste my holiday. I studied a lot. I read more than twenty books. I studied more whenever I felt low or sad. I always reminded myself that I was away from my family for my studies, and that always made me study harder.

Very often, I tried to encourage other students to study hard by reminding them the reason why we all were away from our parents. Many of them would listen to my advice but some of them, especially the younger ones would run away from me.

"Please stop lecturing," said a nine-year student. I used to wash his clothes occasionally. He begged me not to make him emotional. He said my words often made him miss his family in Tibet. I immediately understood him as we all were in the same situation. I didn't dare to make them emotional anymore.

As I grew older, I realized only studying was not enough. I had to be clever, alert and make sure that I had all the documents that I needed to live in the country legally, or opt for scholarships to study abroad.

I had been living in India for years, but technically, living illegally. I didn't have the Residential Certificate (R.C.) that I was supposed to have in order to live in the country legally.

I was in need of my Residential Certificate. Legally, it was almost impossible to get a R.C. as they needed copies of my parents' Residential Certificates. My parents were in Tibet. It was obvious that they didn't have any

Indian papers. Even if they had, it was impossible for me to get copies of their papers. China was censoring, and blocking everything that passed between India and Tibet. I had to find a way to make my R.C.

Bribing the Indian officials seemed the only way to get the R.C. as bribery was the key to everything in India. Bribery was so common that many of the Indians believe it was in their genes to bribe bureaucrats. It was a disease. I am not an Indian, but I had that disease as well. It was the price that I paid for living in India.

Without bribes, a work that could be done in hours could take up to days, and even months. So, I decided to be an Indian and follow their suit. I bought a box of whiskey and headed to the house of the head of the local police.
I pressed the doorbell. There was no response. I pressed the doorbell again, and waited for a few more minutes.

"Yes?" The head of police opened the door.

"Sab je kaise hain?" I respectfully asked him

how he was doing.

"Who are you?" asked the officer.

"Sir, I need a little help," I said.

"What help?" asked the officer.

"I don't have my R.C. and I am wondering if you can help me to get my R.C.?" I said, while handing the whisky box to him.

"Get out, or I will put you in jail," yelled the officer. He almost slapped me. I ran for my life. I was so scared. I took the whiskey box and tried to return the box to the liquor store, but the store in charge refused to take it back.

I stood outside the liquor store, and sold the bottles to a customer at a reduced price. The customer asked me if I stole them from the liquor store. I said, "no" and told him the story. He had a good laugh, and told me, "Giving merely a box of whisky to the head of police office is an insult. You shouldn't have approached him in the first place if you can't give him something better."

That was how I learned that every post had a different price tag. Bribing the head of the police was not as easy as bribing a traffic police officer. I gave up the hope of getting my R.C. Therefore, I missed all the opportunities to apply for scholarships to study abroad as an R.C. was one of the main requirements to be eligible to apply for any kind of scholarship.

Every time, someone who had a lower GPA or academic record than me moved to another country on scholarship, my heart pumped faster, making me punch the walls.

Often, those students whose parents or relatives were in India were able to apply for the abroad scholarships as their parents, or relatives had already obtained the required documents for them to apply for the scholarships. One of my friends who got the first position in our high school final exam somehow got a scholarship to study in London, but he didn't get his documents to apply for a student visa. He had no one in India other than our school, home away from home.

He sought help from every corner, and he did his best, but all in vain. Out of frustration, and depression, he chose to end his life. He hanged himself from a water tower tank. Some said, he had left a note on which he had written that there was no meaning in life. I had never imagined that such a talented, bright student would put everything in jeopardy at the end, but I was able to understand his frustration, his anger and his depression of not being able to get enough love, care and help.

21

My last two years were gone in a blink. I graduated from the school, and joined a leading college in south India. I was studying English literature hoping to become a writer. But English literature was too tough for me. It taught me about the works of other writers but never helped me improve my own writing skills. Exams were tough. I wanted to change my major but I couldn't. If I changed my major, I wouldn't get any financial help from the Tibetan Children's Village.

The only option for me was to finish college. As literature was killing my interest in English, my mind was suggesting other options, and one of the other options was to migrate to Germany as my sponsor with whom I had personal contact was from Germany.

I had contact with another sponsor who considered me as a friend rather than as a sponsee. She had also been paying my school fee, and I loved her letters. She wrote me lots of letters, and sometimes, she would even edit my letters. She would send me gift money occasionally. I once borrowed $ 500 from her to buy a laptop, as I didn't dare to ask my sponsor from Germany to buy a laptop for me. I bought a big, thick, heavy Compaq laptop and I was the only one among my friends to own a laptop. I would lie down on my bed with the laptop on my lap, and spend all of my leisure time chatting, reading, or writing something.

"If you keep your laptop on your lap too long, you will become infertile," teased one of my college friends, who I came to know when we were in high school, and he was anxiously waiting for me to go to sleep, so that he could use my laptop.

"That would be good for me as I don't want to have a baby of my own. I can adopt a baby. There are lots orphans and semi-orphans out there in the world who are in need of love and care," I teased back, signaling he wouldn't be able to use my laptop at least for some hours.

In my class at college, I was the Tibetan ambassador, and I was always bombarded with questions about Tibet, and China. Many Indians knew about Tibet, but those who had never heard about Tibet thought Tibet was part of India.

Occasionally, I, along with other Tibetan students, held free Tibet protest, and drove around with free Tibet banners. Some Indians who had no knowledge about Tibet would ask us, *"kya free melata hai?"*

With a chortle, we would explain to them that Tibet was a country, and we were seeking help to free Tibet, not distributing anything for free.

I did plenty of social work. I taught English to the slum-area children, participated in Free Tibet movements and even helped lots of new students who were coming for college admissions.

Being busy was the best way to kill time, and so I graduated from the college in a blink. I graduated with a degree in
English literature but I felt I didn't learn anything. In contrary, it almost killed my interest in English writing.

After I graduated from the college, I joined another college, one of the best private journalism colleges in India. I studied New Media and graduated with a Diploma in New Media. I got a job at a business news portal even before I graduated from the college, and I joined the news portal following my graduation from the college.

People were right; first jobs are always tough. I didn't last long with my first job. I later joined a Tibetan news portal based in Dharamshala, the head of the Tibetan government in exile. Working with the Tibetan news portal, it opened my eyes to a lot of issues in the Tibetan society.
I realized Tibetans in exile had the tendency of quarreling with each other based on ideological

differences and provinces, and we had been debating about independence versus autonomy for decades.

However, we would all shed tears whenever we heard news of a self-immolation in Tibet. I also learned that all exiled Tibetans whose families were in Tibet were living in fear, and praying that the next news of self-immolation from Tibet was not a member of his or her own family.

22

Kalachakra was the most crowded teaching session that the Tibetan spiritual leader, the Dalai Lama, held normally every five years. I attended one of the Kalachakra teachings in Bodh Gaya, the place where Lord Gautama Buddha was said to have obtained Enlightenment. It was one of the first times I had attended the teachings. I wasn't that keen to attend but the editor of the news portal that I was working for assigned me to cover the ten-day teaching.

There were around 100,000 devotees and 1000 Chinese spies. There were many Indian spies as well. As a journalist, I was able to have access to a lot of facts and figures, which in my opinion many were nothing more than rumors. I wasn't able to track down any of the Chinese spies nor was I able to prove if they really were a threat to the life of the Dalai Lama.

But I loved covering the ten-day-teaching. I made lots of friends, and I even met my other half there. I also found a thick purse with full of dollars. I returned the purse to the owner.

"If it wasn't Kalachakra, I could have become rich," I told my friends boasting how generous I acted by returning the purse to the owner.

"How much money was there inside the purse?" asked my friends.

"Enough to dine with wine and women for a year," I replied.

"Well, if you didn't return the money, you would not have met your life partner." My friends would often joke.

I was not a religious guy other than finding meaning in the teachings of the Dalai Lama, but the whole Kalachakra event was a blessing in disguise. The Kalachakra teaching didn't change my mind much but changed my life. After dating my other half for a few years, I was all set to move to the United State of

America, as she is an American citizen.

When I was in high school, I once wrote a short poem for our school magazine that made to the school assembly board for days.

Thought for the day
--born in Tibet
--grew up in India
--died in U.S.A.
Will you follow his steps?

I wrote the above poem as I noticed many of our teachers and students, nuns and monks were then dying for a visa to the States, as fishes would be in need of water. It seemed I was also going to flow with their steps. It was not just me, but hundreds and hundreds of Tibetans in India were in line, longing to migrate to a Western country. And a number of Tibetans in India who were from Tibet were returning back to Tibet, and my childhood friend, Khando, was one of them.

For most of my childhood, growing up below the Himalayan Mountains at my boarding school in India, I had often looked up towards the Himalayan Mountains knowing my family was just behind those gigantic mountains. The distance was just hundreds of miles. But soon I would be moving further— far, far from the Himalayan Mountains. The distance between my family and me would be thousands of miles. Constantly gazing at my flight ticket to join my other half in the States, I was wondering if the U.S.A is where I really wanted to go. I had promised my family I will return home. So, moving to the west seemed like breaking that promise. A part of me wanted to go to the West but a part of me wanted to return home. My other half was waiting for me in the States and my family was waiting for me in Tibet. I was divided into two. My other half and I decided to visit Tibet before I moved to the States but I failed to get a visa to Tibet. So, I told my parents moving to the West was the only way to get a visa to China, if not to Tibet. My father was convinced. So was my brother, but my mother was still hoping to see me before I moved further away.

I had to see my mom at least once before I moved to the States, and video chat seemed the only way to do that. It was only our hope.

23

Everything was changing, some for good and mostly for bad. The price of vegetables, meat and almost everything in the market were skyrocketing but Internet and phone calls were becoming less expensive. I could call my family in Tibet everyday if I wanted to but only occasionally I was able to reach them. Most of the time, they were unreachable.

"*Duibuqi, ni de dianhua buzai choe*" –Your call is not reachable— was the answer most of the time, but occasionally, I was able to reach them after hours of trying over and over again. Whenever I spoke with my parents over the phone, I sensed both of my parents were living in agony and regret, and my mother would often apologize to me for sending me away to an unknown country. She would always sob. Her agony and her tears would always remind me that the pain in her heart was still an open wound. Knowing my tears would be like rubbing salt into her open wound, I would always calm myself, and hold in my tears. But I often burst out in silence while lying on my bed, drowning myself with tears.

At a time when I was unable to reach them through phone calls, I never dreamed that a day would come where we could do video chat. But after 2010, things were different. We had several free, cross-platform and instant messaging applications where we could talk regularly. And there was the possibility where we could do video chat if my parents or my brother knew how to start or accept a video call. So, I told my family to seek help from someone to make sure that they could come online and do a video chat with their long lost son. We had in fact tried to have a video chat for years but we failed.

For days, I was glued to my bed as my family and I had decided to see each other face to face via video chat. I washed my face. I combed my hair with my fingers. And with my best clothes on, I was just lying down with my laptop on my lap and waiting for my parents to come online. My eyes were motionless, fully focused on my laptop screen as if I was going to enter into the screen. One hour after another, more than six hours passed, my parents still didn't show up. I was not surprised, because that was not the first time where we failed to meet online. I was not that hopeful to see their faces either. The year before, my parents had travelled hundreds of miles from our hometown in order to have a video chat with me but we failed to do that. However, a part of myself was still hopeful. I felt the day I had been dreading was finally coming. From dawn to dusk, I didn't sleep a wink. Apart from constantly rushing to the toilet to pee, I was totally glued on my bed with my laptop on my lap. I could hear the echo of my fingers constantly drumming on the keyboard. My face, rigid with excitement and then frustration, I truly seemed to have aged decades in last two days. At the last minute that I almost knocked off my laptop in anger and frustration, finally the call rang on my laptop. I clicked the green button to accept the video chat. I was suddenly transported back to my family. It was like returning home, but at the same time, I felt strange, as everything had changed in my absence. My three-year-old, younger brother had turned into a young man, much like my father. My parents who were then in their early thirties had turned into much like my grandparents and sadly my grandparents were nowhere to be seen; probably they were waiting for me at the heaven's gate.

My mother, with her toothless mouth wide open, started wailing as if she was going to get a stroke out of crying. My father in his Buddhist monk robe, stood behind with tears racing down on his cheek. He sniffed and patted my mother's shoulder, trying to console her. We were all speechless. Then, my younger brother started speaking.

"Ani?" he said trying to start the conversation.

I turned my head away from them for a minute. I

wiped my tears, and said, "I am going to the United States."

"Then, when would you be able to come home?" said my brother.

"Two more year," I replied as I swallowed the lump in my throat.

"Ga re shey ge dub?" my mom asked my brother while she was struggling to still herself up.

"Two more years," translated my brother. My younger brother was our interpreter. My mother knew only our regional dialect, and I had forgotten our regional dialect.

"Mayang Tsering, khe lama kyab," my mother wished me long life, and requested me to come and see them as soon as possible. I could understand what my mother was saying but I didn't know how to speak in our regional dialect. So, I said, "Yes" to whatever my mom was saying. As usual, she did not say much, she just kept sobbing and apologizing to me.
My dad jumped in and spoke a few words. He was also a man of a few words, at least with me.

Both of my parents were apologetic. No matter, how many times I told them that I had grown up into a fine, educated man, all thanks to them, they were still living in regret and agony.
They didn't say much, just kept quiet, shed tears, and urged me to visit them as soon as possible. "When are you coming home?" was what my mother never missed to ask me, but to their despair, my answer was always, "two more years." For years, I had been giving that same answer.
"Life expectancy of people in our town is short, people are dying around 60s," said my brother, after an hour of video chat, an hour of sobbing and staring at each other.

"Okay," I replied with a heavy heart. What my brother just said was like an icy wind running down through every inch of my nerves, numbing my senses and making me go blind for a moment. With our trembling hands and tears in our eyes, we waved at each other to say "good bye". Within minutes, my laptop screen went black. So was I. Slowly as I gained my senses back, I reflected on what I just saw— my three-year-old younger brother turned into a man, and my parents looked like my grandparents— everything had changed in my absence. It was my foolishness, but I could not let go off of the images of my younger brother as a three-year old toddler, and my parents in their early thirties. I could see my pa in my younger brother and my younger brother in my nephew.

No matter how hard I tried to let go of the past and embrace the reality, a part of myself was still stuck in the past. There was no turning point. The emptiness was always there, I merely hid the nostalgia by masking it with a smile.

24

Returning home was what I dreamed for last fifteen years. I packed everything that belonged to me. I had two bags of books and a suitcase full of clothes. I booked a taxi to the Indira Gandhi International Airport in New Delhi. Within half an hour, I reached the airport. The airport was nothing less than a shopping mall except for the plasma screens of arrival and departure times on the wall of the airport. I stood in queue at the check in desk along with a sea of smiley and cheerful people with suitcases and baggage. I had never travelled in an airplane before and I had never been to an airport either. I was in a state of mixed feelings. Within an hour or so, I was inside the airplane. My seat was by the window and the next two seats between my seat and the next aisle were unoccupied. I sat by the window and buckled my seatbelt. I looked around and everyone seemed so happy. But I felt a rock on my body, so heavy and so cold. My head was falling onto my shoulder. My feet were burning. So were my hands. Every inch of my body was in agony. I even felt my breath was becoming harder and harder. I knew I was not sick, just homesick. I closed my eyes and put the earplugs in my ears.

As the plane took off, the image of myself as an eight-year-old running and shouting whenever I saw plane vapor trails in the sky back in my hometown hovered in mind, and it was a home coming moment. I was back to my hometown, playing with my three-year-old younger brother and feeding our druk-kar making him ready for the sheep fighting festival. My dad was reciting some mantras with a Buddhist prayer wheel in his right hand and my mom was trying to comb my hair. My grandpa was also there, sipping his tea and gazing from our living hall window.

"Drinks." I woke up to the sound of an airhostess serving drinks and snacks in the plane. I knew I just had a dream, but it was so real. Everything was so real. I closed my eyes again, hoping to have another dream but it was so hard to fall asleep. I kept reflecting back over what I saw in my dream. I was surprised how well, and in detail, I could recall and remember about my hometown— the people, the streets and the trees in the neighborhood.

In reality, I was moving more than 7000 miles away from the Himalayan Mountains—far, far from my homeland, but the dream and the reflection about my dream was so real, and so cherishing that I felt much relieved and content to join my fiancée's family in the United States of America.

It was hard to say if I made the right decision to move 7000 miles away from the Himalayan Mountains but it was a good feeling to know another family was waiting for me ahead in the States. And it was hard to say if I would ever introduce my two families to each other ever but I would always remember, the words of the Dalai Lama, "Old friends pass away, new friends appear. It is just like the days. An old day passes, a new day arrives. The important thing is to make it meaningful: a meaningful friend-or meaningful day."

Printed in Great Britain
by Amazon